DRUM ROLL
PLEASE...
IT'S

STEVIE
LOUISE

*This book is dedicated to every
kid who is a bit dramatic.* **T.H.**

For Ben and James. **L.H.**

First published by Albert Street Books, an imprint of Allen & Unwin, in 2021

Copyright © Text, Tanya Hennessy 2021
Copyright © Illustrations, Leigh Hedstrom 2021

Allen & Unwin
83 Alexander Street
Crows Nest NSW 2065
Australia
Phone: (61 2) 8425 0100
Email: info@allenandunwin.com
Web: www.allenandunwin.com

A catalogue record for this
book is available from the
National Library of Australia

ISBN 978 1 76052 641 2

For teaching resources, explore www.allenandunwin.com/resources/for-teachers

Cover and text design by Kristy Lund-White
Set in 11 pt Queulat by Kristy Lund-White
Printed in Australia in March 2021 by McPhersons Printing Group

10 9 8 7 6 5 4 3 2 1

DRUM ROLL PLEASE... IT'S STEVIE LOUISE

ART BY
LEIGH HEDSTROM

TANYA HENNESSY

ALBERT
STREET
BOOKS

ONE

I don't know how many more times I can tell my baby brother to stop riding the cat.

'Riley, off. Get off the cat. Don't ride the cat. The cat is not a horse. He is a sad, old, moody cat who doesn't like people. **GET OFF HIM**. Also, why are you in my room? I know you're only two years old, but respect my boundaries, you feral baby. **I AM TRYING TO RUN A BUSINESS** in here.'

Babies don't understand business. Babies also smell. This baby currently in my room, riding the cat, smells like off milk. Oh, and he's sticky. You touch that baby and you *WILL* need gloves and a mask. He always has a runny nose, even *IN SUMMER*. Why? Grosssssss.

'Stevie, get up. **NOW.** You'll miss the bus,' Mum yells from the hallway. 'Steven, get up.'

My name is *Stevie*. But Mum thinks calling me Steven is funny. She is not funny. She is, in fact, weird. She's going through a phase. A 'there's a crystal for everything', hippy dippy, incense in every room, phase. Mum insists on wearing tie-dyed house muu-muus, which are giant dresses that look like she cut a hole in a bed sheet, put her head through it and called it an outfit.

Last year she made us go to a meditation and yoga course for the summer holidays, as though that's what every twelve-year-old wants to do. Although, it was funny when she farted in the quiet yoga room.

'Steven!!!!' Mum is now at my door. The cat has since run away in fear of its life, so Riley has moved on to chewing on my Maths book. (And honestly, I hope he eats it – I hate Maths.) I'm wrapped in my doona, looking like a burrito. I am *NOT* a morning person. (But I am a burrito person.)

'**STEVEN.** You are going to miss the bus. And if you miss the bus, I will take you to school in the car, and I will get out of the car and wave you off in front of all your classmates. I will yell, *"I love you, Steven Louise. I miss you already, my little joy."*' Mum's really on a roll now. 'It will be embarrassing, Steven. It's my day off today and I'm as free as a bird to embarrass you if you don't get on that bus!'

Mum picks up Riley and pulls a bit of Maths book out of his sticky hands. 'And when you get home you can clean up your bedroom.'

Um. This is not just my bedroom. It's my creative space and temporary office, it's where **THE MAGIC** happens. But yes. Fine. I get out of bed. The thing is, I know Mum really will do all that. She did it last year. It's her hobby to embarrass me. Mum used to be a comedian, so she thinks she's hilarious. I think Mum knows that I secretly think she is a tiny bit funny. But I would definitely not ever tell her that or encourage her by laughing at her jokes.

Mum hasn't done comedy in years. The only person she can make laugh is my dad …and he laughs at insurance ads, so he is an easy crowd. Insurance is really not funny. Dad laughs all the time. If he's not laughing, he's eating. Dad won the local meat pie eating competition. He ate 89 pies. He also vomited up 89 pies…in Mum's car. He laughed about it though. Mum didn't.

· · • ● • · ·

I throw on my clothes and walk into my school shoes. Anytime I'm *NOT* at school I wear my gold boots, but today it's ugly black school shoes. Dad is about to leave for work, and Mum is serving hot dogs for breakfast. Which I don't hate, I just really question why… I told you she's weird. Riley is still smelly and sticky.

My sister Hannah is eating her breakfast hot dog, looking very confused.

Hannah is nine and wearing my hand-me-downs better than I ever could. It's so annoying. I wish I could wear clothes like her. She is fashion. *Farshun.* But she can't spell very well…so all is right and fair in the world.

I've barely sat down to eat my breakfast hot dog before Mum starts herding Hannah and I out of the house.

'Get out to that bus stop,' she says. 'You won't always have such glorious wake-up calls, you know. You'll be off to high school soon enough, Steven!'

When I think about going to a new school and making new friends, I want to get back into my doona burrito. But actually, today is going to be an **AMAZING DAY**, because I have an **AMAZING PLAN** to share with my friends.

Hannah and I have mouths **FULL** of breakfast dog as our ridiculous mother, who for no reason is wearing only one shoe, pushes us out the front door.

'Bye! Love you, Miss Hannah and Steven McStevenson.'

'BYE, MUM,' we say. But then I turn around and say, 'Can we have hot dogs for dinner?'

Mum laughs at my joke, but the real joke is we probably will.

TWO

I live on Brooke Street, which is a tiny street with only five houses. (It's not even a street, it's a cul-de-sac.) One of the houses has been empty for as long as I can remember. It's **DEFINITELY** haunted. One Halloween I was dared to go inside, but I was so scared I couldn't even step on the grass!

But, even with a haunted house, Brooke Street is the greatest street in the world,

because it's full of my best friends. The Brooke Street crew are my everything. I mean, I wouldn't get their names tattooed on my face, but they get me. When they go on holidays with their families, I miss them desperately.

We even go to the same school, which is **AMAZING**. Especially because I'm not my real self around the other kids at school. I get shy and too nervous to show who I really am.

So, let me introduce you to the greatest people you'll ever meet – the Brooke Street crew!

FIRST, the twins. *Macey* and *Luke* are eleven. They live two houses down from me. Macey is the best. She has a bob of white-blonde hair and wears pink glitter glasses. She looks like an actual fairy, which works well, seeing as she's always off with the fairies. She's usually half asleep, in her own world, or all over the shop. Everyone calls her *Spacey Macey*, because she asks the funniest questions. Stuff like 'Does Santa have children? And do elves have families, or do they just work endlessly for Santa? Do they have hobbies? Do the elves get married and have kids?'. The only time you'll see Macey concentrating is when she's on stage. She loves to perform, and is always in the school plays.

Luke is Macey's twin brother. He plays video games all the time, and he **LOVES** YouTube. He's addicted to YouTube. He actually films his own videos, but he's not allowed to upload anything yet. He has sandy blond hair, wears glasses and is always in T-shirts with slogans on them. Like 'I'd rather be on YouTube' or quotes from TV shows. He is so smart and knows a lot about everything. You wanna know something about some almost-extinct lizard? Luke's your guy.

Trixie (real name Beatrix) is twelve – like me – and lives across the road. She has long brown hair and always has it in a braid. **ALWAYS**. I've never seen it out. She uses a wheelchair and can move really freaking fast in that thing. She likes sport. Actually, she loves sport. Trixie is going to the Paralympics one day. For sure. Trixie is so smart too. She tells the best stories and always gets 100% in English. One night we told ghost stories around the fire and Trixie's story was so scary that my sister, Hannah, peed herself a bit. (Maybe I did a little too, but I'm not telling.) And she knows how to make things feel real. Like if there is thunder and lightning in her story, she will turn the lights on and off. Trixie is just that clever, she's one of those people who is naturally good at everything they try.

Alex is ten. He's Macey and Luke's cousin. He is the funniest boy I have ever met. He loves purple, always has nail polish on and loves to sing and dance. He does drama and dancing outside of school. He will sing almost anything. Once he sang the ingredients list of a pack of BBQ Shapes and he nailed it. He loves food. I saw him kiss a bag of Twisties in Year two. Which was and is warranted. Twisties are the best.

Hannah is my sister, which you already know. She is nine and is learning to sew so she can make her own **FARSHUN**. Our nan is teaching her, which is hilarious for me. I have never heard Nan swear so much in my life. Hannah once sewed the skirt she was wearing into the dress she was making. That was a fun day – not for Hannah or Nan, but I got a kick out of it. I wish I was allowed a phone, because that would have gone VIRAL for sure. Hannah doesn't bathe regularly enough for my liking. You cannot pay her to bathe. I tried once.

I saved the best till last, obviously – **ME**. Stevie. **NOT** Steven. I mean, you can call me Steven if you *MUST*, literally everyone does. But my real name is Stevie Louise Mason. I'm twelve years old. I love reading, and watching musicals, TV and films. I like English, **HATE** maths and I **LOVE** acting! I do drama outside of school. At first, Mum made me go. She thought it would help me become the person I am at home and inside myself on the outside too. Like I said, I'm a bit shy – especially at school. But I'm not shy inside. I'm fine with the Brooke Street gang and people who know me. I wish I could be that Stevie everywhere.

THREE

The bell rings as soon as we get to school. Our bus driver, Allan, drives the bus like a snail, so we're always late. Allan does everything in slow motion, it's painful. We could walk faster than the bus goes. He's like a sloth. A sloth who wears glasses, eats ham sandwiches for breakfast, and *APPARENTLY* doesn't know what an accelerator pedal is for.

Before us Brooke Street kids split up to go to our separate classes, I tell them to meet me at the canteen **STRAIGHT AFTER** class.

'And I mean it. As soon as class finishes.' I use my serious voice.

Everyone – even Alex, who is **ALWAYS** late – says they'll be there, and then they head off to their classes. Which is the worst. I hate not being with the crew.

My class is learning about Ancient Egypt, so our classroom is covered in mummies and tombs. My teacher loves craft and a theme, so everything is just a mess of paper and tape and hieroglyphs drawn with textas. We do more room-decorating than book-learning in this class, which I don't hate.

But I *DO* hate reading out loud to the class, which is what Mrs Clark is making me do this morning. Ugh. I don't have any friends in my class. I don't talk much in class, and I think the other kids must think I'm weird. Which isn't me at *all*. I mean, maybe I am a *bit* weird – but I'm definitely not quiet.

Except when it comes to reading out loud.

I mumble a few sentences from the book and hope my teacher, Mrs Clark, moves on to someone else.

'Stevie,' Mrs Clark says, clearly not moving on. 'I heard almost none of that. Go again please, project and be confident.'

The whole class is now looking at me.

I want to disappear.

I read the line again, but I stumble over the words. I'm so embarrassed. (Not as embarrassed as my sister Hannah was when she accepted an award at assembly with her school dress tucked into her undies. But close.)

I try again. **THIRD TIME'S THE CHARM!** I get it all out. But I can't remember what I even said, because I was shaking so much.

Mrs Clark gives me that 'good try' look with her eyes that teachers do. She's nice. I wish I could show her and the rest of the class the real Stevie.

To calm myself down I spend the rest of class thinking about my brilliant plan and how I'm going to pitch it to the Brooke Street kids. I told everyone to meet near the canteen at lunch for my big reveal. (It's best to have very important meetings over sausage rolls and chocolate milk.)

We move on from History to Maths, and although I hate Maths, it means we are that much closer to lunch! I have a knot in my stomach, because I'm so excited to tell the crew about my idea.

Hmmmm. Thinking about it, the knot in my stomach could be the breakfast hot dog.

RRRRRING! Finally, lunch time!

FOUR

I am first at the canteen meet-up spot, as usual. Everyone else dawdles. Except Hannah, who knows when I say 'straight after class when the bell rings', I mean **STRAIGHT AFTER CLASS WHEN THE BELL RINGS**. (I do *NOT* mean seven minutes late, *ALEX*.)

Trixie arrived next, then the twins.

And finally – **SEVEN MINUTES LATE** – Alex.

We sit down in a circle, and my nerves really kick in. I'm sweating, I have a dry mouth and I am *fidgeting*. I can't sit still. I can't even talk I'm so nervous. What if everyone hates my idea? What if everyone laughs? What if they have run out of sausage rolls at the canteen? (The last one isn't related but would still be a disaster.)

I take a deep breath and clear my throat. This is it. 'I have asked you to be here today because, as you know, this is the last year at primary school for some of us, and we're all going to different high schools.' I look over at Trixie, who is going to a sports high. (Obviously, I'm not. I can't catch or throw a ball.) 'Some of you are actual babies and will be staying here.' I give Hannah a sympathetic look. She glares at me.

'Just spit it out, Steven,' says Trixie, eyeing off the handball court. 'You're always so dramatic. We don't need a full-on monologue! Some of us want to play handball.'

'I am offering you all something *extraordinary* here,' I say.

'Unless we all get dolphins that have superpowers, maybe you should limit your use of "extraordinary",' chimes Alex. 'Also, on the topic of extraordinary, are we lunchboxing this weekend?'

I should explain. 'Lunchboxing' is where we tell everyone's parents we haven't had lunch so they will make us lunch, not realising we have been to everyone's house and said the same thing. So every weekend we get four lunches! It's the best.

'Yes, obviously we are!' I say. 'Do you wanna hear my idea or not?'

'Well,' says Luke, chewing on something that doesn't smell like it's super edible. 'The thing is, last time you called a meeting, your idea was for us to clean your bike. What an extraordinary offer for us…'

'Oh, shooooosh. All of you are the worst. That was actually a great opportunity for an enterprising young person. It's not my fault that none of you saw the amazing potential.'

'Steven, please,' says Trixie. 'Get on with it.'

'Fine! Drum roll, please...'

They think I'm kidding.

'No, seriously, Luke – drum roll on your lunchbox, please.'

Turns out Luke has zero rhythm. I make a mental note to ask Trixie next time.

'Okay, so are you ready?'

Everyone huddles in closer to hear, because lunch means kids are playing games and yelling and laughing right near us.

'Wait a second,' I say, holding up a finger. 'Hey! Scram, kiddos! We are **TRYING** to have a **MEETING** here,' I yell at the screaming kids, who have got paint all over themselves. Ah, to be young.

I turn back to the Brooke Street crew. 'So… Here it is… We are going **PRO**.'

Everyone blinks. Macey frowns. 'Like, pro wrestling?'

'Obviously not!' I say. This went better in my head. 'Remember when we did shows for our families at Christmas? That was a **HUGE** success. And I think we've moved on from the amateur scene, don't you? I want to start a performance troupe, and I want you all to be in it! We will all perform together and tour the show around the streets in our suburb and **BEYOND!**'

No one has said anything yet, but I can tell they are getting excited, so I launch into my full pitch. 'Hannah, you can be in charge of costumes. Trixie, you can write the script. Alex, you can do the choreography. Macey, you can do the programs and tickets! Luke, you can do lighting and sound. I'll direct the shows, and of course we will **ALL** be in them! Obviously, we'll have to do a lot of planning and spend weekends rehearsing, but it's going to be **SO MUCH FUN**. We'll get to hang out *ALL THE TIME*.' I wait for their cheers of joy, but no one says anything. They must be cheering on the inside. 'I know.

I'm a genius. I know. These ideas just come to me! What do you guys think? Extraordinary enough? Better than talking dolphins?'

'Yeah, nah. I'm out,' Luke says as he stands up. I knew he would say no anyway. He doesn't want to do anything unless it involves sitting around, gaming and YouTube.

'Come on, Luke.' I feel a bit desperate. It won't be the same if we're not all in it. 'We can sell tickets to our families and friends over school holidays. We can perform at the shopping centres for Christmas. Hospitals? We can do themed shows – like an Easter show! And birthday shows! People will pay us lots of money so that their kids watch us rather than their screen. We will make enough money to go to Disneyland! We will be famous! And rich.' Now I'm definitely desperate.

Luke sits back down. 'Do you really think people will buy tickets?'

'YES!' I am pretty sure. Everyone else takes a beat.

It feels like an eternity.

What is everyone gonna say? Is it a dreadful idea? Did I over sell it?

'YES!' Alex screams. *'Of course I am in!* You know I was born to be on stage, Steven. I love my audience! Remember last year, I played a really funny yet believable Mrs Claus at the low-budget parents-only Christmas show? This will be like that, but better.'

I knew Alex would be in, he is an easy sell. The boy loves the stage, like my mum loves a crystal.

'I'm in, Steve,' Trixie says. 'I can script

and write easily.' She starts edging towards the handball courts. 'Um, can I go now?'

'Yes, go!' I tell Trix, even though she's already gone.

'I'm down!' says Hannah. 'Making costumes will be good experience for my fashion resume. Hannah Mason, Costume Designer. It's got a ring to it!'

'And you'll act, too, right?' I ask.

'I guess so.' Hannah shrugs. 'But I'll obvs be making myself the best costume, suckers!'

Macey takes longer to answer than I thought she would, but she eventually says, 'Obviously I'm in! I love drama and acting and drama.'

'Did you say drama twice? Also, Macey, is your jumper on backwards and inside out?' I ask.

'Yup,' she says. But doesn't do anything to rectify her jumper situation.

She is especially **SPACEY MACEY** today.

· · · ● · · ·

I can't believe it! Everyone (except Luke) is **IN!** Everyone (except Luke) is **HYPED!** No one more than me! *EEEEE!!!!* **THIS IS HAPPENING!**

'Okay, everyone,' I say, 'planning starts *TONIGHT*.'

FIVE

'**NO WAY,**' Mum says when I get home from school. 'You will be doing your homework, not holding a "business planning meeting". Also, the living room is a mess and so is your bedroom. And,' she says, trying to stop Riley from eating her earring, 'I might add Steven, you're twelve, you can't run a real business.'

Wrong, Mother, so very wrong. Well, not wrong about the mess in the living room. (Riley is like a hurricane – he can turn a room from liveable to bomb site so fast he could offer it as a service.) However, she is wrong that this isn't a real business.

'You can have the living room from ten until twelve tomorrow,' she says.

'This is **SERIOUS**, Mum. I'll need heaps more time,' I explain.

'Well, you'll need to be more time-efficient, Miss Business Lady, because I am having some friends over for book club and cheese at twelve, and I will need you feral children out of the house.' Mum pulls her earring out of Riley's sticky reach. 'Riley, stop eating my jewellery. These were expensive.'

'*Fine,*' I whinge.

Mum is right, but I don't want her to know I think she's right. If I want to pull this plan off, I need to be focused. Mostly, I need to make sure we don't just let Alex talk about his love of *Grease* for four hours like we did last weekend.

At least now I have time to make an agenda for the meeting. An agenda that doesn't include *Grease*. I will have to fight Hannah for the computer.

· · • ● • · ·

I am so bored all Friday night that I clean the bathroom and reorganise my room. Now that I'm a professional theatre director, my room needs to look more adult. More professional. I shove my toys into the bottom of my wardrobe, because there's no way I'm throwing them out. I might need them for props! Obviously.

· · • ● • · ·

On Saturday morning, Mum announces that breakfast is Coco Pops and broccoli. She says it's 'for balance'. I told you she's weird. It tastes so bizarre. Dad is laughing and taking photos for Facebook, which he calls Bookface even though **HE KNOWS** it's Facebook. Ugh.

But nothing can bother me this morning – not even Mum's Coco Broco Pops – because I am wearing my **GOLD BOOTS**.

My gold boots were a present from my favourite person, *my pop*. My pop told me that when he was a kid, he was really shy too. (Apparently, we are really similar except I'm not 80, I don't have a beard, and I don't have dentures...yet. I think Mum means our personalities.) When he was a kid his dad got him a pair of shiny brown leather boots, and infused all his luck, confidence and bravery into them. They made him feel invincible. Pop thought gold boots were more my style, and he put all of *HIS* luck, confidence and bravery into my boots! Anytime I wear them my shyness disappears, and I can do anything! Which is why it's such a bummer that I'm not allowed to wear them to school. That would solve at least 94% of my problems.

'Hey, Steve, your brother is trying to kiss your cat's bum,' Trixie says as she wheels in. (Trixie is always on time, which is just another reason why she is the **BEST**.)

The first time we started spending weekends together, all the parents realised our houses weren't accessible for Trixie. They were pretty embarrassed, so now we all have ramps up to the front door, and wheelchair accessible bathrooms. I wish all houses were just like that already.

'I know. Riley is obsessed with the cat,' I reply.

Macey wanders in behind Trixie. 'Before we start,' she says thoughtfully, 'I need to know... Who do you think invented words?

And how come *zahpit* isn't a word? Can it be a word? Who do I have to ask to make it a word? Who allows words to be words?'

I think about adding it to the agenda, but settle for saying, 'Let's Google it later.' Because now I wanna know.

'Riley is trying to wear the cat's tail as a scarf,' Hannah says, bringing a tray of four whole carrots, eight single sultanas, three bananas and a jar of vegemite to the table.

'This isn't Cheezels, Hannah,' Alex says, eyeing the tray from the doorway. 'You know my rule. Cheezels, bare minimum. I don't work for free.'

'I know, but this is what Mum gave us.'

'I love your mum, but—'

Hannah throws a sultana at Alex.

'Okay!' I say, in my most director tone. 'Let's get down to business. Item one on the agenda is **CHOOSE NAME**. We need to think of a name for our performance group!'

'Let's call it **Broadway Babies**,' says Alex with jazz hands.

'How about **Plays and... Stuff**,' suggests Macey.

'Hmmmmmmm, maybe **Brooke Street Players?**' says Hannah.

'Oh, what about **Lights Camera Action!**' Trixie adds.

'Or what if we call it... Your baby brother is licking the cat,' Alex says.

'Too niche,' I say. 'No one will get it.'

'No, Riley is literally licking the cat.'

WHAT IS WITH THIS BABY HARASSING OUR CAT?!

'*MUMMMMMMM*,' I shout. 'Riley is in here licking the cat again.' I try to shepherd Riley out of the lounge. 'Shoo, go on. Get out of here you feral beast baby.'

'I'VE GOT IT,' Alex says. 'Let's call it *Lunchbox* because we always lunchbox on the weekends.'

'Ooh, I like it!' **FINALLY** some good ideas. 'Although, it needs to sound more grown up. What about Lunchbox *Productions*?'

'I hate it,' Luke says, sauntering into the living room, frowning at the tray of strange snacks.

'Well, *you're* not in the group, Luke,' Macey says. 'We love it.'

'What are you guys even gonna do? Plays? Music? Dancing? What?'

'That's the *next* item on the agenda.' I am about to hand Luke an agenda but then stop. 'Why are you here? You said you didn't wanna do it.'

'Cause I love you guys! You are my only friends. I'm sad without you. I missed you.'

Luke is the worst liar in the group, if not the whole world. 'Why are you *REALLY* here?'

'Mum turned off the Wi-Fi,' Macey and Luke say at the same time.

'Well, if you're gonna be here shhhhh your

mouth, Pukey Lukey,' Macey says.

Luke scoffs and sits down. 'What have I missed?'

'We're planning the first show,' Alex says, through a mouthful of half-chewed banana. 'I think we should do a puppet show. Ooh, or a twist on a classic? Maybe something like Peppa Pig the Musical? Oh, we could do Grease! I already know the s—'

'NO,' everyone else says at the same time.

'What about a One Direction tribute play?' Macey asks.

'Let's do a **variety** show,' Trixie says. 'Then we can all do something different.'

'A circus show?' Hannah says.

'None of us have any circus skills,' Alex replies with a huff, dipping the banana in vegemite.

'Well… I mean, I can do magic? I can make a whole jar of Nutella disappear!' Alex winks.

We all cry laughing.

'Wait, who are we performing this for?' Luke says, interrupting our laughter with logic. 'That will help us think of what the show will be.'

'Did you just say **WE**, Luke? Are you back in?' I ask.

'It depends on a few things,' he replies.

I know the only thing it depends on is whether or not the Wi-Fi is on at his house at rehearsal time. Even though it's not the serious passionate commitment I was hoping for, I'll take it.

'Luke's right,' says Trixie. 'Who is our audience? It can't just be our parents again, right? You said it was going be **BIGGER** than that, Stevie! Where are we performing?'

'Where, Stevie?' asks Hannah.

'Where, Steven?' asks Alex.

'Where, Stevie Louise?' asks Macey.

Luke looks at me and chews a carrot.

Uh oh.

The Brooke Street kids have always done dancing, singing and terrible comedy in the backyard for the parents at Christmas. But I wanted to do something bigger and bolder and better. Before we're all at different schools, I wanted to make sure there would be something that kept us all together.

But I forgot the most important thing. Professional shows need professional venues.

Everyone is looking at me.

I feel sick. My cheeks are hot.

'It's…uh…' I wiggle my toes in my gold boots and feel a little bit braver. *'It's a surprise!'* I say, smiling my biggest smile. 'Now please turn to page two of your seventeen-page agenda.'

Look, I'm not *technically* lying. It *will* be a surprise.

To all of us.

Because I have **NO** idea!

SIX

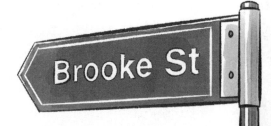

I wake up on Sunday morning with a funny feeling in my stomach. I can't stop thinking about the show, and how I'm going to make it happen. This show is the only way to make sure the Brooke Street crew stay together. And we *have* to stay together.

'Steven,' Mum yells through my bedroom door, 'we are going to see your nan and pop this morning. Don't make me beg you to get ready.' There's a quiet thump outside the door. 'And can you dress Riley?'

Uugghh.

'I will dress Sticky,' I say, opening the door. 'But you should know that I have changed his name to reflect his grossness. Riley will now be known as *Sticky Grosstown*.'

'Well, he is sticky, so I can't argue with your logic. Just dress Sticky and yourself, and I will meet you and Hannah at the car. We are already late.'

Nan and Pop live in *the Peach Centre*, an old people's home not far from our place. It smells weird there, but I don't mind.

I love my nan and pop. Their house has so many pictures of us as babies and toddlers. Sometimes I look at pictures of me when I was younger and think, what was Mum thinking making me wear that? Socks and sandals?

Really, Mum?

Pyjama pants and a sequin top? A nice dress and a Superman cape? Actually, on second thought, I think I dressed myself that day.

And every picture after that has me in my gold boots, so obviously *I look amazing*.

The other best thing about Nan and Pop's place (besides Nan and Pop themselves) is the lolly jar. Nan has to refill it every time we go over. I am more lolly than person when I stay at Nan's.

· · ● · ·

We finally get to Nan and Pop's house and knock and knock…and knock. Nan is out, and Pop has a bad leg so it takes an eternity for him to get anywhere. I hear my pop bellow/

sing 'coming, guys, I'm coming…slowly'. My pop is the best. He's a singer and used to be a radio announcer. He also used to tour around old people's homes until he got too lazy and got really into Neighbours. Pop is always singing. It drives Nan **UP THE WALL!** He is like me. I drive Nan up the wall, too.

Pop tells us that Nan is in the common area at the old people's house. She's running late from doing a hip-hop dance lesson.

WAIT, WHAT?
NAN'S DOING HIP-HOP?

I tell Pop I will go get Nan. For him, but also for me. Because I **NEED** to see Nan doing hip-hop dancing. I need see **MULTIPLE** nans dancing to Snoop Dogg. I hope I haven't missed it, and she's just caught up talking to the other nans about things old people like, like watching daytime TV, drinking coffee at a food court, and eating dinner at 4:30pm.

But when I get there, I am **THRILLED** to discover that I am not too late. Nan is NOT chatting about being old. She is doing a full *CHOREOGRAPHED* performance with the other nans. Now I really want you to **VISUALISE**. Rihanna's *Umbrella* is playing, and it is **LOUD**. There are fourteen nans dancing. All of them have grey and white set hair. Some of them are wearing bedazzled backwards caps. All of them are twerking. The *NANS* are **TWERKING!** There is so much hip movement for people who have had them replaced. *It is* **AMAZING**.

The young teacher is nailing it. The nans are…ummm…trying their best. They look like they are having fun, which I guess is the point?

As if twerking nans isn't life changing enough, I see something out of the corner of my eye. Something miraculous.

There's a community noticeboard in the corner and it has a pink piece of paper tacked on it. It says:

> ### ENTERTAINMENT WANTED
> The Peach Centre is looking to expand its repertoire of performers.
> Do you know any entertainers?
> Musicians, singers, poets, plays...anything.

It's like everything goes into slow motion. The heavens open up and a light shines on the ratty noticeboard in the Peach Centre.

THIS IS IT. *THEY WANT ANYTHING?* **WE CAN DO ANYTHING!**

This is a *PROFESSIONAL GIG* for a real **AUDIENCE**.

Then I read more:

> *PAID.*
> *Contact Jude at reception.*

PAID! *THIS IS THE* **BEST DAY** *OF MY LIFE.*

Before I get the chance to wrap my brain around everything, my sweaty nan comes over and hugs me from behind.

'Stevie Louise! My *beautiful* grand-daughter! Oh, I'm late, oops! I was really into that hip-hop class. Did you see me krumping and twerking?'

'I don't think I will ever be able to un-see it, Nan,' I say, laughing.

'The dance teacher says I'm very limber for my age, Steven. I may be back-up dancing for Beyoncé next year! You never know!' Nan lets go of me and wiggles her hips. 'Okay, let's go home, my sweetness!'

Back at Nan and Pop's house, Nan serves cake and I pretend to listen to Pop's story about a rabbit he saw on the lawn, but all I can think is **PAID. PROFESSIONAL. GIG.**

I tighten the laces of my gold boots and decide to call Jude as soon as I get home.

SEVEN

I can't focus at school on Monday. We had a test on Australian geography and I wrote *Dunno* instead of *Dubbo*.

Q: Where in NSW is the Taronga Western Plains Zoo?

A: Dunno.

It would be embarrassing, except that it's funny. I want to tell **EVERYONE** in the class about it. But I'm not wearing my gold boots, so I'm not brave enough. I just sit there instead.

We have a Brooke Street meeting at lunch again. There are two items on the agenda:

1) I wrote *Dunno* instead of *Dubbo*.
2) I have **NEWS**.

· · · ● · · ·

'Guys, you will never believe what has happened!' I say as the crew gathers near the canteen. Then the wind picks up, and my nose starts tingling. 'Wait. Macey, what is going on? Why do you smell like that?' I ask.

'I didn't have my glasses on, and I accidentally used hairspray as deodorant and deodorant as hairspray. So my arms are stuck down from the hairspray and my hair is powdery and smells like flowers. I look like an old lady,' Macey says, sounding pleased.

SPACEY MACEY.

'You are an icon,' Alex says.

'Speaking of old ladies,' I say, butting in. 'Want to hear my news about the show? My surprise?' *I can barely hold in my excitement.*

'Oh yes!' exclaims Alex. 'Tell us, girl!'

'It better not be our parents' backyard!' Hannah says, picking at the tomatoes with sprinkles Mum packed for lunch.

'It's **NOT** a backyard,' I say sharply. 'It's at the Peach Centre.'

'Oh, what's that? Is it a new theme park?' Alex says, getting excited.

'Is it a fruit shop?' Trixie asks, tossing a tennis ball into the air and catching it over and over. I know she wants to throw it to someone but no one else in our group can catch. Which is embarrassing, but also really funny.

'Is it a peach lovers event? Do people go there to just love and praise peaches? Because I love peaches. I could support that!' Macey says.

'Wait,' Hannah says, frowning. 'Are you talking about the old people's home where Nan and Pop are?'

'Yes! Although, it is a *retirement community*,' I say in my most excited voice.

'Are there actual peaches there?' Alex asks.

'Ah nope... But heaps of dentures and old people!' I say.

Everyone is silent, clearly in shock at how brilliant it is.

Then Trixie says, 'Ah… An old people's home is…well…old.'

'The Peach Centre was built only five years ago. It's a cutting-edge facility. I know because I read the brochure ten times while I was waiting for Nan to have her hair done one time.'

Suddenly, I'm nervous. *What if they don't want to do it? What if an old people's home is an awful idea? What if—*

But then Macey chimes in, in her fairy way, 'Well I, for one, think this is **HUGE!**'

'You know what? Same!' says Alex. 'This is a great gig! Can you deal? It's a real thing now! I love this for us.'

'You're right,' Trixie says. 'This is amazing.'

'I kind of can't believe it,' Luke says.

'Steven, this is actually happening!' Macey says excitedly. 'When are we booked in? How long do we have to rehearse?'

'Five weeks! And it's paid,' I say.

'*Paid?* **WHAT?!**' Alex says.

Maybe I should have led with the fact it was paid, not that it was at an old people's home.

'Oh my god!' Alex continues. 'At ten years old, I will be a professional showman. I am living my dreams! **THIS IS EVERYTHING!** Maybe they will put me on the *cover* of *Woman's Day*?'

'It's $140, between us,' I say.

'**AMAZING. $140 THAT'S SO MUCH MONEY!**' Alex says.

I could see him spending the money in his head.

'We have to entertain people for thirty whole minutes,' I say.

'Steven, I'm scared,' Hannah says. 'This is huge. These are real people, not just our parents and a few cats.'

'Don't be scared! It's going to be *AMAZING*,' I say. 'We just need to come up with an idea for a show for old people. What do old people like?'

Trixie looks thoughtful. 'Soup? Gardening? Bingo? Getting knee replacements? Soft biscuits?'

'The news? Fancy plates we're not allowed to touch?' Macey says.

'Old people love history,' Luke says.

'You know what old people love? **A CLASSIC**,' Alex says. 'We could do *Les Misérables*? Or *Hamlet*? Or *Phantom of the Opera*? Or *Grease*?!'

'**NO!**' we all say together.

'I've got it!' Trixie says. 'Let's do a **NEW**, funny and cool *Cinderella*. I can write it!'

'*YESSSS!*' shouts Alex. 'I am playing the wicked stepmother. Can I? Don't bother answering, I'm doing it! It's cast, thank you, see you, bye,' Alex says.

'Trixie, you're a genius!' I say. 'How soon can you write it? We need to start rehearsing, like, yesterday.'

'I'll do it this week!' Trixie says, finally putting the tennis ball down.

'So,' I say, 'it needs to be a thirty-minute show, a **TWIST** on the classic of *Cinderella*, something with a beginning, a middle and an end. And maybe some songs?'

'Consider it done!' Trixie says confidently. 'Mum got me some script-writing software, so I can make it look totally real.'

'Perfect!' I can't wipe the smile off my face. 'Rehearsals start Monday, everyone!'

This is happening. *This is HAPPENING.* It's all coming together! This is going to be easy!

EIGHT

'**L**ess chatting, more rehearsing!' I yell. 'And Alex, I don't think the stepmother needs a tiara and a wand. She's not a fairy, she's a villain!'

'Well, it's my choice as an actor, and I choose to be in a tiara and have a wand. I am a villain with a tiara and a wand.' Alex points the wand at me. 'I look great. Read the shirt, Steven. I am **ICONIC**.'

He's right. I can't argue with him.

The rehearsal space (our backyard) is chaos. Everywhere you look there is mess and noise. There are Brooke Street kids in half-finished costumes, reading scripts, Macey is designing programs, Trixie is telling my mum about her inspiration for her work. And as always, my traumatised cat, *Cat*, is running from Sticky. (I should have told you earlier, the cat's name is Cat. I named him when I was one.)

Mum said we could do the show if Hannah and I did our homework, unpacked the dishwasher, set the table and cleaned up after Sticky *without complaining* for the whole five weeks until the show. It's been a week, and it is **HARD**… I'm good at drama, but I excel at whinging and complaining!

Mum also said she was proud of me for taking my drama classes seriously and being brave enough to perform a **REAL** show. And I am proud of me, too! We have a venue, a cast, a script and an audience, **AND** I get to spend the next few weeks rehearsing and performing with my best friends.

When Trixie decided to put a spin on *Cinderella*, I didn't think she would make it so strange. But trust me, it's **REALLY STRANGE**.

Alex is the wicked stepmother. Trixie and Hannah are the ugly stepsisters who also play the fairy godmother and mouse. I am Cinderella. Macey is the prince.

We thought Macey might be cranky that she had to play a boy, but she didn't mind because the prince isn't a boy – he is a seal. The prince is a seal.

Yes, you read that right.

In *Cinderella*, the prince is a seal.

Like a dog of the sea. A seal.

Did I mention it's set underwater? Told you, **STRANGE!**

The fairy godmother is a lobster, the evil stepsisters are dugongs (which Hannah says are a nightmare to do costumes for), the wicked stepmother is whatever Alex feels like doing, and Cinderella is human. (Mostly because Hannah went as Cinderella for Book Week and we already had the costume, which goes perfectly with my gold boots.)

We called it *Cinderella: SEA WHAT HAPPENS*. The title was Dad's idea, and it's not the worst. I don't mind a pun. Plus, it sounds like a *real* theatre show.

LUNCH BOX PRODUCTIONS

Cinderella
SEA WHAT HAPPENS
by Trix

TOP SEA CRET

A dream is a wish your heart makes

Luke finally agreed to join the show for real, although he refused to act in it. He is doing the *tech side* of stuff. He seems genuinely excited. He's trying to get his hands on a smoke machine, to make the set look 'legit underwater'. (Yes, I know there's not much smoke underwater, but I'm trying to be a supportive friend...)

I'm nervous and stressed, but I feel good. Even with Luke doing the lighting and sound, I still have to organise the rehearsal schedule, plan catering, do set design and stage managing, make props... Plus, direct and star in the lead role! I'm nervous and stressed, but I know it will be worth it. As long as I've got my Brooke Street crew and my gold boots, I can do anything.

What could possibly go wrong?

NINE

Okay, so a few things go wrong.

We put on a play reading for the parents, and they have a lot of questions.

Questions like:

Why is it set underwater? (Trixie had just watched a shark documentary.)

Why does the lobster fairy godmother have a French accent? (Honestly, I have no idea.)

Why does the wicked stepmother have a British accent? (Alex made a bold choice and really went for it.)

Why does the wicked stepmother have two songs and no one else has any songs? (Alex demanded it.)

Why is prince charming a seal? Of all the sea animals, you went with seal for the prince? (Great question, Mother, I agree.)

Why are the ugly stepsisters wearing such nice outfits? Aren't they ugly? (Hannah is doing the costumes and wanted to design and wear something she liked, and she likes nice things. She did say she would be making something amazing for herself.)

Why does the opening take place in slow motion? (It's dramatic and they did it in Hamilton.)

Why is there no pumpkin carriage? (You refused to give me a budget for a giant pumpkin, Mother.)

Why does Cinderella wear gold boots if she is poor? (I'm not even answering that, I mean honestly.)

They also have a lot of feedback.

Mum – the ex-comedian now suddenly drama teacher – says, 'Steven, you can't just throw it together. It has to make sense. Needs to be a bit more cohesive. It needs *light* and *shade*. You have to commit!'

'We are committed, Mum! There's just so much to do. I wish someone else could play my role or I had a less full-on role…'

It's overwhelming trying to do everything!

Then Mum says something truly ridiculous. 'Steven, darling, if you want me to be in it, you only need to ask. I'm expensive but worth it.'

NO WAY was I going to let Mum be in the show, but she was right. It is kind of a hot mess.

But it's *OUR* hot mess.

Sure, it's hectic and I'm doing fifty million things all the time. But it's also so much fun!

And we are basically ready to go.

Well, kinda. Sorta. **_Not really._**

Okay, so I guess we aren't at all ready.

But Macey has finished the programs, and Macey and Luke's mum is going to print them at her work.

We did headshots like the programs in real shows. We took the photos on Alex's older brother's iPhone. Most of the headshots had filters on them, which I was mad about at first. You can't do a professional show with

Alex as the wicked stepmother

Macey as the seal prince

a headshot of you with dog ears and a dog tongue hanging out (Alex!), or with huge alien eyes (Luke!), or love hearts and butterflies (Hannah and Trixie!).

But I forgive them. They just aren't as professional as me.

And even though rehearsals can be stressful sometimes, we are all closer than ever. Normally sleepovers would be watching musicals and playing games, but now it's line runs. Trixie is frantically changing the script every minute. Even Luke is all in, making sure we have the best sound effects and that the music is perfect. He is practising the cues over and over!

Hannah is using a stapler for costumes like it's going out of fashion, but everything looks pretty slick! Especially considering our budget is around $32 and a quarter of a donut.

But **UGH**, don't even get me started on the budget. That's the worst part. Hannah and I are doing extra chores for money so we can pay for the costumes and set pieces. We have to pick up the cat's poo and iron Dad's work shirts and wash the car.

I have a feeling this show really worked out more for Mum than us. She's loving the spare time so much she's joined a contemporary ballet class for adults! (She's swapped the muu-muu for a unitard. It's a lot on the eyes.)

I am doing the rehearsal schedule and making sure we have everything we need! I have never made more lists in my life. I am the list queen at this point!

Most afternoons after school we practise. It's always fun, even when Alex yell-cries

at us when he is performing his songs and we're not paying 100% attention.

One afternoon, when we are rehearsing the scene when the ugly stepsisters try on the shoe, the most hilarious thing happens.

I can't find the prop shoe, so we use the *cat* instead. Macey 'tries it on' Trixie and Hannah's feet. And they all played it so sincerely, which made us laugh even more.

'This shoe is fluffier, fartier and more cat than I remember,' says Macey. 'But if it fits, it fits, and I'll be queen!'

It sent us. We fell into a pit of hysteria and laughed for two hours straight. We laughed so hard Alex and Hannah peed themselves.

Then we had to wash their pants and start rehearsals again. Which was *super gross*.

Alex wet his pants twice that day.

Cat meanwhile is so over it he doesn't even care anymore.

It is so fun just hanging out and doing something we all love.

That is, until **DOOMSDAY**.

TEN

It's two weeks until the show, and I know it's going to be a terrible day when I am woken up offensively early (7:30am, which is so *RUDE*) on Saturday morning by the **BEEP BEEP BEEP** of a truck reversing. And by an epic thunderstorm – lightning and thunder and everything.

I can mostly block out the storm, I can

almost block out the truck, but I *CANNOT* block out the people yelling! Who is yelling this early on a Saturday?

'Careful with that, it's glass,' says someone.

'Darling, please hold Ava while I supervise the bedhead. And when is the fridge getting here?'

I look out the window and see the strangest thing. There is a big moving truck parked outside the house next door – the fifth house on our street, the house that is 1000% haunted! One time, we tried to get Mum's friend Kira, who is a psychic, to go over and see if there were ghosts in the house. She couldn't be bothered, because she was having a wine and cheese with Mum, **BUT** she did say, 'Oh yeah, there are probably ghosts'. And that was all I needed to know that there were definitely about 8000 ghosts residing there.

But today *PEOPLE* are moving in! Living, breathing, not-ghost people!

What?! **NO WAY.** There hasn't even been a For Sale sign on the house... Now all of a sudden, a family is moving in!

I wonder if they know that there are ghosts in there? Should I tell them?

The Brooke Street kids are gonna lose their minds when they find out ghost house is going to have people living there.

I watch people running in and out of the house with furniture in the rain. I can't believe it. New people are moving into OUR cul de sac.

'Steven!' Mum calls out. 'Breakfast! We're having bolognese sauce on Sao crackers.'

Well, it's better than hot dogs. But not by much.

· · · ● · ·

Whilst shovelling the Saos in, I tell Mum about the new neighbours.

'Oh, how nice!' she says. 'Once the rain dies down, we will go say hello.'

Ahhhh, excuse me, Mother. **I DO NOT WANT TO SAY HELLO TO THEM!**

What I want to say is, 'Hi, this house has 390 ghosts, they will haunt you in the most annoying way, like eating all your Tim Tams and changing the channel just when the show gets good. You can leave now. Goodbye.'

But that doesn't happen.

· · · ● · · ·

Once the moving truck is gone and the rain stops, Mum drags us all over to meet the new family.

The mum looks fancy and smells even fancier.

Sticky isn't used to mums who wear perfume (mum wears a crystal rock deodorant) and starts to cry.

The dad seems okay, even though he makes too many dad jokes for my liking. Jokes like:

'What happens when you go to the bathroom in France? European.'

'I'm so good at sleeping I can do it with my eyes closed!'

And his favourite, which he said five times in the twelve minutes we were there was, 'I'm on a seafood diet. I see food and I eat it.'

Hannah and I *rolled our eyes so many times* I worry we will have to see an optometrist later in the week. My dad, however, is in heaven. He has found his soul mate.

Then we meet *her.*

I knew straight away I didn't like her. She has long blonde hair and giant green eyes and looks way too friendly. Suspiciously friendly.

'Hi, I'm Addison,' she says. 'It's so nice to meet you all! Thanks for swinging by to say hello.'

Addison talks like a Disney princess, practically singing as she speaks. I look around to see if there are any tiny birds or cute mice nearby, who may or may not be able to sing or tie her hair up in ribbons, but it's just us.

'It's our pleasure. *Welcome to Brooke Street!*' Mum says. 'You have such lovely manners, Addison. Steven, Hannah, doesn't

Addison have lovely manners?' Mum says in a pointed tone.

I roll my eyes. 'Hi, I'm Stevie. My name isn't Steven. I am not a 60-year-old mechanic going through a divorce. Nice to meet you too, Addison,' I say, trying to appease my mother, while also trying to be funny.

Addison doesn't laugh.

No one laughs.

Well, Hannah snickers.

Addison has a baby sister, Ava. She's the same age as Sticky. And they have a cat too. It's called Maple. *Ughhhhhhhhh.* Even **THE CAT** has a Disney name. I bet Ava doesn't try to lick Maple all the time.

Then, the worst thing I've ever heard comes out of Mum's mouth.

'All the kids in the street are doing a performance for the local old people's home,' she says. My stomach drops. 'Addison, do you like drama? Do you do any acting or singing?'

No, no, no.

'I do,' says Addison excitedly. 'I love drama! At my old school, I did drama at school and after hours. I even did a commercial for a car company when I was little, and a Kit Kat commercial. I want to be an actress when I grow up.'

'Oh great,' says Mum. 'You'll have to be in their show then!'

EXCUSE ME, WHAT?! SINCE WHEN ARE YOU THE CASTING AGENT, MOTHER?!

I quickly butt in before this can get any worse. 'Oh, that won't work. We go on in

two weeks and we are basically finished. Maybe next time?'

'Don't be silly, Steven,' Mum says. She turns to Addison. 'Steven was just complaining that the show was going badly and she really needed someone to play her part because she wanted to concentrate on directing.'

Thanks, Mum. I shoot a look at her. She isn't looking at me. I hope she can feel my death stare.

'Oh, Addison can learn lines very quickly,' Addison's dad says. 'She has a great memory on her. Not like mine! I've got the memory of a fish!' Addison's dad does a truly horrendous impression of a goldfish, which would be hilarious except I am too furious.

How is this happening?! I feel out of my body, out of control. I don't know what to say or do.

'Well, we all know how hard it can be to make new friends in a new town so we'd love to have Addison involved,' my mum says.

No, **WE** wouldn't, Mother!

Mum is still avoiding my death stare and keeps talking. 'The kids are rehearsing this arvo in our backyard. Pop around and they will slot you in!'

Addison starts talking excitedly but I can't hear her over the buzzing in my head.

SLOT HER IN! HOW?! WHERE?! WE ARE PERFORMING IN TWO WEEKS! FOURTEEN DAYS! IT IS CAST AND ALL BUT FINISHED. IF ADDISON JOINS, WE WILL HAVE TO START AGAIN!

Mum knows I'm angry because I am staring her dead in the eyes and she's giving me a purposely blank look.

'Great idea, Suzette,' I say through gritted teeth. Mum hates it when I use her first name. 'Thank you so so much for organising that.'

'That is so kind of you both!' Addison's mum says. 'Addy will see you this arvo.'

After the parents take about a hundred years to say goodbye, we walk back to our house. My eyes are so wide with disbelief that my eyeballs almost fall out.

Hannah looks as shocked as I feel. She mouths, **'*WHAT ARE WE GONNA DO?*'**

I have **NO** idea.

ELEVEN

I had a whole speech planned. I was going to tell the Brooke Street crew about Addison. Something like, 'Thank you all for coming, and I'm sorry that my mum has ruined this play and possibly our whole lives.'

And then they would riot, and they would refuse to talk to Addison, and I would just have to tell Mum that it isn't going to work out. What a shame.

As we are sitting around getting ready for another run through, I clear my throat loudly. Here goes. 'Thank you all for—'

Mum bursts into the backyard with Addison in tow. 'Here is the gang! I'll let Steven introduce you to everyone!'

'Thank you **SO** much, Mum. You have been a dream today. I love you,' I say, with as much sarcasm as I can muster. Which is **A LOT**. And she knows it.

None of the Brooke Street kids knows this stray child. They look at me, then at Hannah – who shrugs unhelpfully – and then back at Addison. Before I get a chance to explain, Addison jumps in.

'Hey, I'm Addison. I just moved in next door. Stevie's mum said I could be in your show. I'm so excited!' She's so confident. I can barely introduce myself to one new person, let alone four!

Have you ever seen four people's jaws

drop simultaneously? I have. I wish I could have filmed their reactions. They didn't say anything out loud, but I know them so well I can read their little minds.

Here is what is going on in their heads:

STEVEN'S GONNA FLIP.
IS THIS SERIOUSLY HAPPENING?
WHEN'S LUNCH?
NOT LOST

It takes Addison 45 minutes to convince the group that, yes, she actually did move in next door, and no, she isn't a ghost who had adopted human form. Then we move on to the issue of the show.

'So, the thing is, Addison,' I say, 'the show is really already finished, and we don't have any spare roles.  I don't want to be rude, but clearly it's too late to add you in. Plus, we have already printed the programs.'

'Oh.'

Addison looks deflated. 'Okay...'

I knew she would find logic and understand. This show is for the Brooke Street crew. **MY *Brooke Street crew*.** I will have new people to deal with in high school soon. I'm not ready to do it yet!

'But maybe next year?' I say.

'Oh, I get it.' Addison turns to leave. 'I'm sorry for interrupting rehearsals. See you later, maybe.'

'Come on, Steven,' Trixie says, holding Addison's arm. 'I think we can add her in!'

I shoot a look at her. This is not the plan.

'Yeah, we can add you, girl,' says Alex, gently. Which is rare, because Alex is like a bull in a china shop. (No seriously, he's banned from **SEVERAL** antique shops, true story.)

The Brooke Street kids gather around Addison like she's Ariana Grande at a meet and greet. They ask her every question ever. I mean *EVER*. Macey even asks what time she was born!

I am smiling and trying very hard not to scream.

Mum pulls me aside. 'Stevie, you of all people know how it feels to be left out and how hard it can be to make new friends.'

Mum is using her Mum Voice. Ugh, she is right. But I am still torn.

'Mum, you don't get it! We have basically finished the show and now you want to add someone last minute? She probably can't even act!' I know I am being rude and mean, I can hear it. But I don't know how to stop.

Mum gives me a stern look, and I know she's about to put her foot down. 'If Addison isn't in the show, you're not doing it, Stevie Louise. Period.'

WORST. DAY. EVER.

TWELVE

Addison is holding court with Alex, Macey, Luke and Hannah. She tells them about the car commercial she did and what her old school was like. Trixie and I spend the rest of the day trying to figure out how we can make it work.

It's not like I hate Addison and want to exclude her on purpose. I just feel a bit...

scared. Scared that everyone will like her more. She is so confident and friendly, and she's had **REAL** acting jobs. The rest of the gang seem to really like her already.

'Steven, focus!' Trixie waves her hand in front of my face. 'Maybe Addison can be the fairy godmother lobster? Hannah didn't want to act at the start, remember?'

'Yeah, but Hannah is so good as a lobster fairy. Maybe Addison could be the prince's butler, who is a seahorse or a walrus or something?' I suggest.

Trixie frowns. 'I don't think that will work, Steven.'

UGH. I turn to the group and say, 'Here's what we're going to do. Addison, we'll perform the show for you, and you can tell us what you think, and where you could slot in.'

'YES', says Alex. 'Hannah, did you polish the tiara?'

· · · ● · · ·

We perform the full show, and Addison claps and congratulates everyone. It is definitely better since our last run though with our parents.

'Oh my god, this is so good. I'm so, so impressed! This is the real deal!' Addison looks genuinely happy. 'This is **REALLY** good! It's so funny! I love that the prince is a seal! I'm so glad that of all the places we moved to was onto a street with a professional drama group!'

'Thank you so much, Addison, you're the best,' Alex says, puffed from his performance.

Alex is beaming from Addison's compliment, and he deserves it. He really is amazing. 'I know we just met, but I already love you!'

'Stevie,' Hannah whispers as she pulls me away from the group, 'maybe Mum was right.'

Excuse me, what?

'Now don't lose it, Steven,' Hannah says carefully. 'But what if Addison took over your role? She looks a bit like Cinderella, and you're already doing so much. It might just make it easier? Lighten your load!'

EXCUSE ME, WHAT?

Are you kidding? Are. You. Kidding? **ARE YOU KIDDING?!**

I turn back to the group to tell them what my traitor sister said. 'Everyone, Hannah thinks that Addison should be Cinderella!'

I laugh.

No one else laughs.

Trixie says, 'That's not a bad idea actually! It will take some pressure off you, so you can focus on directing.'

'But I—'

'Don't worry, Stevie, you're still in the show!'

says Trixie. '**OBVIOUSLY** you're still in the show, but Addison can play Cinderella, and I'll write you in as Cinderella's funny sidekick. You're so good at comedy parts anyway, Stevie.'

SIDEKICK?!??!?!?!?!

What is happening?! This whole thing was *my* idea and now my best friends are replacing me with Addison – a **STRANGER**.

'Yes, that could work,' Macey says.

'I think that would be brilliant! I can see it now!' says Luke. 'Stevie you are better at comedy. Plus, it makes no sense that you're in gold boots all the way through, when Cinderella is meant to be in glass slippers and stuff.'

'BUT,' I say loudly, 'Cinderella doesn't have a sidekick! It won't make sense.'

'Steven, it's set underwater! It doesn't matter!' Trixie says. 'It's just a funny story loosely based on a classic. May I remind you that **THE PRINCE IS A SEAL?**'

'Beatrix,' I say, looking into her eyes. She knows I'm upset because I'm calling her by her full name.

'Oh, I couldn't do that!' says Addison. 'It's Stevie's show. I can't take the title role!'

'You have more *acting* and *performance experience* than any of us!' Hannah says. 'And your dad says you learn lines quickly!'

'I have a **REALLY** good memory,' Addison says, 'so learning lines is easy for me. **BUT** I don't want to upset everyone, especially not you, Stevie! I can just be an octopus in the background.'

'Ah Addison, you are **NOT** octopus-in-the-background material.' Alex turns to me. '**STEVEN**, I think this would and could be **ICONIC**. Don't you agree?' Alex is patting the cat, *Cat*, and looks like a real evil villain – in a tiara, with a wand.

'So, Stevie,' Hannah says, probably fearing for her life. 'What do you think?'

Everyone is staring at me.

Addison is smiling at me. *UGH*, she is **SO NICE**. She even smells nice. She was moving into a dusty house all morning and we have been hanging all afternoon. How does she **STILL** smell nice? The rest of us smell like rotten eggs. (Especially Alex. He goes **HARD** when he performs. Sweats everywhere.)

'Yeah, sounds great,' I say through gritted teeth and a fake smile. 'We can do that.'

Everyone cheers, but I feel like crying.

Why does everyone love this girl they **JUST** met so much? We don't even know if she can perform and we're going to put her front and centre of our show? Oh sure, she's done *ONE* Kit Kat commercial – which I've never seen, by the way!

More importantly, what if she turns out to be a **REAL** weirdo who owns 24 ferrets?

'Stevie, your role will be **AMAZING**, I promise,' Trixie says, pulling me back to reality. 'I better go work on the script. So excited to have you in our Brooke Street team, Addison.'

'Thanks, Trixie!' says Addison, high-fiving her. 'Oh, are we still on for handball at your place tomorrow?'

Of course Addison is good at sport too. What can't this child prodigy do?

I keep my fake smile stuck on and try not to panic. How did I go from confident and ready to spiralling out of control?

Oh, I know… **ADDISON**, queen of the ferrets (probably).

THIRTEEN

It is three days out from performance day, and things are **TENSE**. Not the group, just between Addison and me.

Well, really just me.

Addison is seriously getting on my nerves! She keeps making us do drama exercises before rehearsals and everyone loves them. Everyone loves everything she does. Everyone loves her.

Except me.

I don't love her. I think she's annoying, and she is **CONSTANTLY** making 'suggestions'.

'Stevie, you need to project your voice more!'

'Stevie, is there going to be a green room at the venue? Will we have dressing rooms?'

'Stevie, do you want to do some trust exercises?'

'Stevie, should we start today with vocal warm-ups?'

'Stevie, should we do more physical stuff?'

'Stevie, I need to go home and feed my ferrets. Would you like to come?'

I KNEW IT! I KNEW SHE WAS A FERRET PERSON!

· · ● · ·

The only good thing about this is that Trixie wrote the most **BRILLIANT** part for me. I'm meant to be the comic relief, and truthfully, I am hilarious. I am also a jellyfish.

Hannah as fairy godmother/ stepsister 1

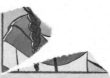

Trixie as mouse friend/ stepsister

Stevie Louise as ick Jellyfish

Addison as Cinderella

The show starts with Cinderella scrubbing the seafloor with Spray 'n' Wipe. (I thought we didn't need to have Cinderella using Spray 'n' Wipe underwater, but Trixie said we should

be open to brand sponsorship deals. Told you she's a genius.)

Alex, as the wicked stepmother, steps on Cinderella's hand and lets out a dramatic sigh. 'I'm not sorry, Cinderella, your hand was in the way of my foot.' Alex points his foot and waves it in Cinderella's face. 'If I'm walking you need to move. *I'm* the queen. You're a peasant. Also,' Alex says, throwing a Cheezel on the floor and standing on it. 'You missed a spot, babe.'

Then once the wicked stepmother leaves, I – Cinderella's sidekick jellyfish and hype girl in her imagination – enter and say, 'Cinderella, all you do is clean! Do you wanna sneak out of the palace and get KFC?'

COMEDY. GOLD.

· · • ● • · ·

We do another practice performance for Mum, and she **LOVES** it. Mum says the show is better with Addison in it. She also says it's better for me, because I can just be funny and leave the boring bits to Addison. She is right, and I even almost tell her so.

But then she says Addison's experience and professionalism raised the bar and made us all better, so I'm glad I didn't tell her she was right.

Addison has not 'made us all better', Mother! She has **RUINED** my play and **STOLEN** my friends.

Although she does let me play with her ferret during rehearsals. His name is *Tripod*, because he has three legs.

Tripod is now my only friend.

Yes, I know I'm dramatic.

FOURTEEN

I wake up on the morning of the show and throw up.

I am beyond nervous. I can't eat. I can't concentrate. I can't do anything.

The Peach Centre has advertised our show as 'young people's theatre' and we were billed as 'the evening show'. The show starts at 4pm.

The *evening* show is at *4pm!* That's firmly 'afternoon' if you ask me!

All of the Brooke Street parents help pack the costumes, props, set pieces and the epic smoke machine into the car. It is really cool that Luke took his job seriously – his dad found an amazing smoke machine on eBay and it only needs water and just plugs into the wall! Plus, the smokey haze makes it look underwater! We look professional!

As we are packing all the costumes into the car, I realise I can't find my gold boots.

I look everywhere. **EVERYWHERE**.

They aren't at the end of my bed, where I keep them. They aren't under my bed. They aren't in the living room. They aren't in my parents' room. They aren't anywhere.

My breathing starts to get heavy. I can't go on without those boots. There is no way. No how. Never. I cannot. I run back into the living room to check under the couch again.

'Mum!' I shout, on the brink of tears. 'Have you seen my gold boots?'

Mum comes into the room, with Sticky on her hip. 'Yes, I washed them, to have them all ready for the show today. I wanted them to look perfect…'

Relief takes over my body. 'Oh, thank goodness. I was freaking out I had lost them!'

Mum kneels down gently next to me. Mum is never gentle, that's not her vibe. Suddenly, I know it isn't gonna be good news.

'Stevie, when I washed your boots for the show, the colour came off.' Mum puts her

hand over mine. 'They are still the same boots, but they're white now. I'm so sorry, my darling.'

'Oh.' My face feels hot and I want to throw up again. 'I can't go on stage without them, Mum.'

'Yes, you can! Stevie, sweetheart, you don't need the boots. You are you, and you are brilliant and funny and wonderful. The boots are just boots.'

Mum doesn't get it.

They are more than just boots. They are my good luck charm, my superpower. They make me brave enough to do anything!

And without them, I can't do the show.

Addison will have to go on solo. She knows all my lines. She knows everyone's lines. She will be great.

'Stevie,' Mum says, 'you love performing. You'll be great even without your gold boots, because **YOU** are great.'

I am so upset, but I know Mum is trying to help. Besides, she looks as upset as I am.

I think about my nan and pop, who are so excited for the show, and all the old people who are coming. I think about the Brooke Street crew, my best friends. Weirdly, I think about the twerking nans. That makes me feel a bit better.

'Okay,' I say, as a tear rolls down my cheek.

I don't know how I'm going to do this.

FIFTEEN

We are performing in the Peach Centre Hall, the same room where Nan does her hip-hop class. There was no proper stage, so our parents made some long and tall 'wings' to indicate the side of stage so we had somewhere to be 'backstage'.

We use the toilets as dressing rooms. The

Peach Centre Hall has six toilets in separate rooms – which is lucky for us, otherwise we might have been doing a quick change while Mavis goes to the bathroom.

'Do you want the props set up, Steven?'

'What do you think of this, Steven?'

'Where are my lucky undies, Steven?'

Everyone is asking me 1000 questions. None of which I can answer. Without my boots, my head is somewhere else!

It is an hour before the show when we finally finish setting up the theatre. Well, I say 'we' but I mean 'me, Trixie, Luke and our parents'. Addison's mum called my mum to say they were running late from dance class, but would be here 'pronto'. *UGH.* Alex spent the time walking around the space and introducing himself to objects in the room in character. Which was the weirdest thing to endure. And Macey just asked us every question under the sun about old people. She even asked some of the old people who had arrived **VERY** early.

'Why do old people smell like old people?'

'Can you bottle old people smell?'

'Is the fountain of youth a real thing?'

'What happens if you put a baby in the fountain of youth?'

Finally, Addison arrives with her mum and dad.

'Oh, wow this looks so good! I can't deal with how great this is! You're all amazing!' She walks in like she's Lady Gaga, and everyone in the Brooke Street gang rushes over to say hello. *UGH.*

But it gives me a chance to sit backstage, away from everyone, to think and breathe.

Everything feels like it's happening too fast, it's too much. I feel so lost without my boots.

I feel like crying again. I want to cry about my ruined gold boots, and about how I'll never be brave again.

Suddenly, the stage curtain twitches and Addison's head pops through.

'Stevie, do you know where my—' She stops.

I quickly wipe away a few tears. 'Do I know where your costume is? Yup, it's with mine backstage! Hannah steamed them. They look great.'

I wish Addison would just go away. Instead, she sits down next to me.

'Are you okay, Stevie? What's wrong?'

'Nothing,' I say, even though clearly something is wrong because my face is red and wet.

'Lies!' Addison says. 'You can tell me.'

She is the **LAST** person I want to talk to! Literally the last person on earth. But she gives me an encouraging look and I think maybe I do want to talk to her.

'Mum washed my gold boots and now they are not the same.' Just saying it makes a few tears fall. 'The boots are my confidence, they

make me, me. I can't go on without them. You have to go on without me, Addison.'

I thought she would be elated by this news. But she isn't.

'No!' Addison says fiercely. 'I won't go on without you. You have got this! You don't need them! Stevie, you're amazing. You're so funny and smart and determined. The show needs you. I need you!'

I was in shock. I thought she hated me. 'Really?'

'Yes, absolutely.' Addison nodded quickly. 'You're a star! I've never met anyone so cool. Stevie, you're so unbelievable! You know what you want and you go after it, and never take no for an answer. When you get knocked down, you get back up again! You organised a **REAL** show for a **REAL** audience. And it's the most amazing thing I've ever seen!'

I mean, she's not wrong. I really did do all that.

Addison's not finished. 'The world needs to see you perform, and this weird-smelling old people's home is just the beginning!'

'You don't know how much those boots do for me Addison,' I say. 'They make me shine.'

Addison scoffs. 'You weren't wearing the gold boots at your parents' anniversary party last week, and you did that amazing improv performance of "Stacey the retail worker". Everyone was in hysterics!'

IT WAS VERY FUNNY.

'And last week,' Addison says, 'you took them off because it was *50 degrees* during rehearsals and it was your **BEST** run through! You also weren't wearing them when you made a speech at Trixie's surprise birthday pool party when you rapped and rhymed *"sports"* with *"shorts"* fifteen times. That was hilarious and so brilliant.'

'Thank you, Addison,' I say, suddenly

sobbing for a different reason. 'It's really nice of you to say all that.'

'You haven't ever really seemed to like me,' Addison says softly, 'which has been hard, because I think you're so cool. I wish I was more like you!'

I think I'm still in shock. I can't be hearing this right. Addison, perfect Addison who everyone loves and wants to be friends with, wishes she was like **ME?!**

'I really like you, Addison!' I say. 'I'm so sorry I made you feel like I didn't. I was worried that my friends would rather be

your friends than mine, because you're so confident and cool. Honestly, I wish I was more like *YOU!*'

Addison squeezes my hand.

'*THANK YOU*, Addison.' I breathe out. 'I feel so much better.'

'Okay, let's get ready!' Addison stands up. 'We have thirty minutes till show time, and—'

'And we need to do a vocal warm-up,' we say together.

SIXTEEN

The audience files in, taking their seats and chattering away. It's the slowest entering of people ever, because they are old. It's like they are the ones under the water. Macey's programs are a hit, and everyone thinks having most of the headshots with filters and half of them upside-down is 'so hip'!

A lot of people are in wheelchairs and some are even in beds attached to breathing machines and heart monitors and stuff. But they want to see the show so bad, they bring them in anyway!

They all look like my nan and pop – it's literally a room full of nans and pops. I can hear my actual nan and pop telling everyone that I am their granddaughter and that I am a creative genius and a star! I can also hear them talking about Hannah and her amazing

costumes. I can hear Pop from backstage because even though he's super old, he can talk louder than anyone with a microphone. I sneak a look out from the side curtain and see them showing everyone pictures of me and Hannah. Mum really needs to print new photos for them though. I'm twelve now and a pic of me nuddy in a bath when I was three isn't going to help them recognise me now!

And it's maybe a bit weird for Nan to be showing people, let alone have them made into a T-shirt, which she has also done.

NAN!

• • • ● • • •

It's five minutes before we go on!

I am sweating, like I-might-need-a-new-costume sweating. I am so nervous and still worried about not having my boots. Then I remember my pop saying, 'being nervous means you care, it's a good thing!' and what Addison said, that what makes me shine isn't the shoes, it's **ME**.

· · • ● • · ·

I'm not sure when I became Addison's biggest fan, but I'm okay with it.

· · • ● • · ·

The lights dim. Luke is absolutely nailing it.

The opening music starts.

The audience goes silent.

I look at Alex, who is on the opposite side of the stage to Addison and me. He winks at us and mouths 'chookas', which means 'good luck' in the theatre. Then he snaps his fingers and mouths, 'This is **EVERYTHING**. I love you.'

Alex takes a big deep breath and walks onto the stage.

It's happening! **IT'S HAPPENING!**

This is it! The beginning.

SEVENTEEN

Alex absolutely **OWNS** the stage as the wicked stepmother, and his English accent is perfection. He winks at the crowd at the end of the opening scene and leaves the stage.

Oh god, this is my moment. My first scene as Cinderella's sidekick jellyfish slash hype girl. I walk onto the stage.

'Cinderella, all you do is clean!' I think about projecting my voice. 'Do you wanna sneak out of the palace and get KFC?'

The audience is silent, and I think I might be sick.

Then they go wild with laughter. They **LOVE IT!**

Soon it's my favourite scene, the night of the Underwater Ball.

'You think you're going to the ball?' says the wicked stepmother. 'In that mess? I don't think so, babe. The ball is for hot people in hot outfits. You're not hot, Cinderella, and

neither is that outfit.' Alex adjusts his tiara. 'The ball is for icons. You're not an icon.'

'But I got a dress,' Cinderella says.

'No, babe.' Alex points at Cinderella. 'You and a mouse hot glued some old tea towels together. That is not a dress, that is a **MESS**. You can't go to the palace in that. You will embarrass the family.'

Trixie, an ugly stepsister dugong, says, 'Yeah, don't embarrass the family, Cinderella! I never embarrass the family.'

Luke presses the **fart sound effect**, perfectly on cue and the audience loses it.

I am supposed to be looking like a sad jellyfish sidekick, but I am laughing, because it is so brilliant!

The wicked stepmother and ugly stepsisters start chanting, 'You can't go, you can't go, you can't go!'

Then Alex shouts, '**WAIT!** Maybe we are being too mean?'

The chaos stops. After a perfectly timed pause, Alex says, 'LOL kidding! You can't go!'

They all throw their heads back and do the best evil cackle and start tearing off Cinderella's tea towel dress in slow motion, while we play Billie Eilish.

It looks **AMAZING**. Trixie is a genius. We are all geniuses.

The audience **LOVES IT**. They laugh at all the funny bits, they gasp at the dramatic bits. They even clap at one point, in the middle of the show, which was unexpected. And meant we had to pause for clapping! We hadn't rehearsed that.

It is all going **SO WELL**.

Until it isn't.

EIGHTEEN

The Seal Prince – Macey in a grey beanbag – is about to arrive at the ball.

The Underwater Ball is the big moment for the smoke machine, but there is nothing happening.

I gesture frantically to Luke from backstage.

He looks panicked for a second, but then he quickly sneaks out through the audience to the back of the hall where the smoke machine is sitting.

Luke messes with the power plug for a moment then gives me a discreet thumbs up.

He sneaks back to his lighting desk and the smoke machine starts working right away.

It looks **AWESOME**.

The ball has **ATMOSPHERE.** (Or hydrosphere, I guess?)

That is, however, the last awesome thing that happens…

A loud beeping sound suddenly takes over the Peach Centre Hall. Like, **REALLY** loud.

The audience starts murmuring and looking around. But we are **PROFESSIONALS**, so we keep going, saying our lines extra loud.

Cinderella has just gotten to the ball, when suddenly all of the normal lights come on and three nurses run in.

'It's Arthur!' one of the nurses says.

They run towards the back of the hall.

We stop.

The show doesn't go on.

We are all on stage now. Me, Addison, Alex, Hannah, Trixie and Macey. Even Luke is standing up at his lighting desk.

Everyone wants to see what is going on.

The nurses gather around an old man's bed.

· · • ● • · ·

So, imagine this.

There is a **SERIOUSLY LOUD** beeping sound.

There are three nurses clustered around a bed.

There are fifty really old people in a big hall.

And there are six kids on stage – one is a seal, one is a lobster, two are dugongs, one is Cinderella and one is a jellyfish.

'His heart monitor is unplugged,' one of the nurses says.

I look over at Luke, frozen at his lighting desk.

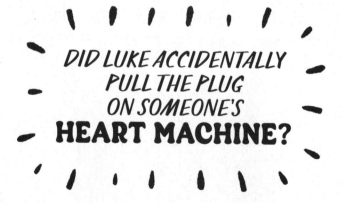

DID LUKE ACCIDENTALLY
PULL THE PLUG
ON SOMEONE'S
HEART MACHINE?

THE MACHINE THAT MAKES HIS HEART BEAT?

DID WE UNPLUG THAT FOR THE SMOKE MACHINE?

ARE WE MURDERERS?!

NINETEEN

'What do we do?' Addison whispers to me.

'I have no idea,' I whisper back as we stand uselessly on stage. *We didn't rehearse for this!*

Luke joins us onstage and I put my arm around his shoulders. Hannah holds his hand with one of her lobster tongs.

And then, just as our parents storm the stage, the beeping stops. The man in the bed sits bolt upright, looks at us on stage, looks at the smoke machine and looks back at us.

'They unplugged my heart monitor to plug in the smoke machine?' he wheezes.

There is a pause.

'THAT'S HILARIOUS,' he says, laughing.

The crowd erupts with laughter. Everyone is doubled over laughing! Have you heard fifty old people laugh? It's the best! The nurses, staff and paramedics start to laugh too.

All of us on stage start to laugh too. Except Luke, who might be crying as well as laughing.

'I'm sorry, sir, I'm so sorry,' Luke says to the man in the bed.

'It's more than okay, young man. I used to sing on stage, and I would have done the same thing. There's no business like show

'business! And the show must go on!' The old man grins at Luke. 'What's your name?'

'I'm Luke!' Luke says, looking relieved. 'Do you still sing?'

'My name is Arthur,' the old man says. 'And no, I don't sing anymore. I rap!'

'Really?!' I exclaim. This is even better than the twerking nans!

'No!' Arthur shouts, laughing so hard he wheezes again. 'But I really was a singer, and I know a song everyone will know. How about we close this show with a song?'

'Yes sir, sounds good,' I say.

The nurses wheel Arthur's bed to the centre of the stage and prop him up with pillows so he can sit upright.

Arthur is clearly an old hand, and he takes to the stage so easily. He's pretty lively for someone who we thought was almost dead five minutes ago!

'I'm okay!' he shouts, and the crowd cheers. 'What a great day we have had here at the Peach Centre. We loved having the Lunchbox Productions gang here... Even though they tried to kill me!'

Everyone laughs, and Arthur winks at Luke. Luke looks like he might be sick.

'How about we end this afternoon with a song and a dance?' Arthur says.

The crowd cheers again. They are ready for it!

· · · ● · · ·

So, imagine this.

There's an old man in a hospital bed on centre stage, leading us all through an acapella rendition of 'Greased Lightning' from the musical Grease.

Alex is absolutely loving it, 'cause, Grease. He has never looked so happy!

There's a lobster fairy godmother and two dugongs doing the Grease moves.

The twerking nans are getting the most out of their hip-hop lessons and their new hips.

This has got to be the weirdest, wildest, **MOST AMAZING** day ever.

TWENTY

It is a strange feeling as we pack up all of our props, costumes and left-over programs. (Macey thought 600 programs would be appropriate for a fifty-person audience. *Spacey Macey* strikes again.)

PROPS

Luke picks up the smoke machine and says, 'I think we gotta get rid of this. Do you think Arthur might want it?'

Everyone laughs. Partly because it really is funny to think Arthur would want a souvenir, but also because none of us can quite believe what happened today.

· · • ● • · ·

Our parents are super proud of us, even with the attempted murder.

'That was amazing!' Addison's dad says. 'Everyone loved it. Sure, we didn't get to see the end, but it was so wonderful.'

I didn't know he could get through a sentence without a dad joke. But I guess he can!

'Hey, Stevie, I know you love my jokes.' He winks at me.

Ah, I guess he can't. I do my best go-on-but-make-it-quick smile. 'I sure do!'

'Why do melons have weddings?'

'I don't know. Why *DO* melons have weddings?'

'Because they can't-elope!' Addison's dad laughs. 'Get it?! Can't-elope! Cantaloupe!'

I groan out loud and look at Addison, rolling my eyes. She rolls her eyes back to me and groans too.

At the same time and in the same tone, we say, 'Ugh, dad joke!' And burst out laughing.

Addison's dad is still laughing at his own joke. My dad joins in and they high five each other like it is the best joke in the world.

· · ● · ·

Suddenly, Jude from the Peach Centre runs towards the stage.

OH NO. She is going to be mad at us!

There's going to be yelling.

I turn to Addison. 'We're doomed! No one will ever hire us!'

Addison squeezes my hand. 'It's not your fault, Stevie! We all did our best!'

'Miss Stevie!' says Jude. 'Where is Stevie?'

Everyone points at me. *THANKS A LOT.*

My mum comes over and puts her arm around me.

I brace myself for the worst.

'Oh, Stevie!' says Jude. 'We have had the best feedback on the show!'

Sorry, what? I am so stunned I can't say anything.

Jude keeps going. 'It's the best entertainment we have had here in years. Everyone loved it. Can we book you guys again?!'

Book us **AGAIN?!**

'Seriously?!' I say. 'Even though we almost killed someone?!'

'Oh, Arthur is fine,' Jude says, waving her hand. 'But we didn't get to see the end of the show, and everyone wants to know how it ends. We would love to see the whole thing again!'

I can barely keep up with what Jude is saying.

'And if you have any other shows you're working on,' Jude says excitedly, 'we would

love to see those too! And I'd love to let the other nursing homes know how great you all are!'

'*Huh?*' say Luke and Macey in unison.
'**WHAT?**' Mum says.
'*Oh. Em. Gee!*' Alex says.
'**NO WAY!**' says Addison.
'**POO,**' says Sticky.

'Yes, we can do that!' I say, finally catching up. 'Yes! Definitely! We would love to! Thank you so much!'

'I will call you and set it all up,' Mum says to Jude.

· · • ● • · ·

Macey, Luke, Trixie, Alex, Hannah, Addison and I do a big group hug onstage before leaving the hall.

What a day.

WHAT A SHOW.

'I love you guys!' Hannah and I yell out the window of our car as we back out of the Peach Centre carpark.

'Love you, too. We did it!' Trixie yells out from the passenger seat of her mum's car.

'Love you all!' shouts Macey, and I'm **SURE** Luke says it too, under his breath.

'We are icons!' screams Alex, surely waking every person in the Peach Centre. It is 7pm, so they are definitely in bed, because old.

I briefly wonder how Alex is going to wash out all the glitter he put in his hair and all over his face. But that's an Alex problem.

I fall asleep on the way home, even though it's only a ten-minute drive. Hannah says I fell asleep smiling.

TWENTY-ONE

So here is where this story gets strange. You're probably thinking how could it get stranger? Well, we went viral. Like, **REALLY** viral.

We were featured on the national news, TikTok, Facebook, YouTube, every news website *AND* every radio show.

I know I'm *dramatic*, but I'm ***not exaggerating***. We were even on TV in America, because Luke had set up a camera to record the show and posted it to his YouTube channel.

Luke asked us and our parents' permission before he uploaded the video. And he asked Arthur, too. Arthur was **SO EXCITED**. (He wants front row tickets to our next show.)

Everyone wanted to talk to the kids who could have killed an old man during a show!

Calls were flooding in from people wanting to book Lunchbox Productions. Mum was answering all the calls and dealing with all of that. She was loving it, and kept calling herself a 'talent agent'.

· · · ● · ·

At school, we were famous. And for the first time, it felt like everyone knew the real me! The one dressed as an imaginary jellyfish.

I turned my *not-so-gold* boots into pot plants. Dad helped me put holes in the bottom for drainage, and I filled them with dirt and planted cactuses in them. **They looked cool.** I could have sold them at the markets for at least $50. But I didn't. I gave one to Addison and one to my mum, to say thank you and sorry. I didn't need the boots anymore.

· · · ● · · ·

The weekend after the show, we lunchboxed hard, because we had a **NEW** house to lunchbox. Addison loved it. It was the best weekend, eating way too many lunches, laughing at what happened, hanging at Addison's house and trying on all her shoes, playing Uno and dressing up Tripod in a suit and tie.

I just wanted to be *twelve* for a bit, and hang out with the Brooke Street crew **WITHOUT** all the stress of a show.

Best friends first, famous performers slash creative geniuses second.

I went to bed early on Sunday night, straight after dinner (scrambled eggs and Nutella). I felt satisfied, not by dinner (obviously), but in my heart. I felt amazing.

· · • ● • · ·

But when I wake up for school, Sticky is in my room. Again.

I DON'T KNOW HOW HE KEEPS GETTING IN!

Oh god, he is painting the walls with Cat's poo! *IT IS EVERYWHERE.* Some is in his **MOUTH! OHHHH THIS IS FERAL!**

'*STICKY!!!* You rank baby! GET OUT OF MY ROOM! MUM!' I yell. 'MUM! Sticky is painting the walls of my room with poo. Get out! Out, Sticky! I know you're only two, but I am running a very successful theatre company in here.'

I guess some things
never change.

Until next time.
Stevie OUT.

THE END.

ACKNOWLEDGEMENTS

Thank you to every author who made me love reading. Your stories made my childhood magical. Your words helped me escape into lands beyond me: Morris Gleitzman, R. L. Stine, Paul Jennings, Robin Klein, John Marsden, Ann M. Martin, and Louisa May Alcott – thank you for Jo March, a brave and fearless young woman.

To my mother, who made me read, which made me write – thank you for giving me the joy of reading. Even though I didn't always want to, I'm really glad you made me!

To my nanna, Pat – thank you for reading me stories as a child. I remember lying in your bed in New Lambton, and you would make up wonderful tales about Penelope. I think about those memories so often. Thank you for giving me the joy of your time and endless love.

Thank you to all my high school teachers for teaching me the skills to articulate the thoughts in my brain. In particular, my high school English teacher, Jan Boswell. All teachers should aspire to be like you. Thank you. Sincerely.

To Scott Allan – when I was fourteen, you came and spoke at our school. You told me to never have a back-up plan. That way the only option I have is success! I'm glad I listened. I miss you. Thank you.

Thank you to the publisher of this book, the kind, visionary and wise Susannah Chambers, and the editor, the brilliant, smart and creative Matariki Williams. And of course, the illustrator of Stevie Louise, the 'literal genius' Leigh Hedstrom. You managed to get inside my head and make these characters look exactly how I imagined them. Working with you was one of the most rewarding partnerships in my career. Thank you for helping bring Steven to life!

I also want to acknowledge: Jack Lonsdale, Zara O'Sullivan, Jake Woods, Jamila Rizvi, Rosie Waterland, Tom Poole, Alanna Hennessy, Kevin Hennessy, Daniel Hennessy, Lena Barridge and Pete Helliar.